MURDER ON VIDEO CHAT

— ⁂ —

SAIRAH BASHIR

CONTENTS

1

— • —

THE MURDER

The world stops. Bedrooms become offices, or prisons. Or both. All kinds of people willingly or unwillingly confine themselves to these offices/prisons. Lawyers. Accountants. Hairdressers. Chefs. Actors.

Actors like Chloe and Max. Their precious late teenage years bleed away in their shoebox apartments, as they forcibly rehearse their upcoming sketches through their low pixel quality video chat.

"That was a, uh, a good rehearsal," Max stumbles at the end of their session. Worrying thing is, he stumbles even through lines he doesn't need to memorise.

"Yeah, see you same time next week?" asks Chloe, her cute smile glistening through the camera.

"Uh, sure, see you then. Uh, bye."

And, just like with every video chat, there's that awkward smile at the end and the waving of the hand, each person desperately waiting for the other to end the call and make this awkwardness end.

So it finally does. Max leaves the video call. Chloe's teeth vanish behind a frown.

"That was a, uh uh uh, a good rehearsal. Yeah, right."

Chloe rolls her eyes, about to exit the video chat herself, when she hears the PING of an email notification.

She departs from the video call. "Please don't be Max, please don't be Max."

Chloe enters her inbox. Her well-groomed, perfectly symmetrical eyebrows rise up to her forehead. "Anisa?"

She clicks open the message.

No writing. Nothing. Just a photo attachment.

She double clicks on the image...

The screen stains in blood. Blood that trickles down Anisa's lips, as she sits lifeless in her chair, eyes wide open.

Chloe's scream pierces the air.

***

"No I've not had an accident, but you'll get into one if you call this number again, understand?!"

That's me. Gordon Findlater. And no, my last name is not pronounced like 'find later'. I don't 'find things' later. I 'find things' quick. And I have to. I mean, it's my job to find things out quickly.

Otherwise I wouldn't last that long as a detective.

Okay, back to the bit where I was screaming at an annoying cold-caller. After shouting and cursing the guy I slam the phone onto the desk, and return to my computer screen where I'm on video chat with my goofball colleague Derek.

"Hey Gordon, what you think of this new background?" he asks, as his clean beige wall transforms into the bloody milky way.

"You're not in outer space! Though sometimes I wish you were."

"What you said?"

"Nothing."

Derek decides to literally come back to earth.

"Sorry. Uh... Gordon?"

Derek looks serious (for once). "What is it?" I ask him.

He holds up his right hand...

"What hand am I holding up?"

"Really?"

"Come on, tell me."

"Your right hand." Obviously it is.

"You mean the hand on your right side or mine?" he stupidly asks.

"Does it matter?"

"Just tell me."

"Your right side. My left."

"I don't get it, why-"

"You're looking at your mirror image!"

"What? So I'm looking at my mirror image and you're looking at me..."

"The right way round."

"Right?"

"I mean, the CORRECT way. The way people see you in real life."

"That's so weird."

You're weird. I say in my head.

I almost have the urge to say it out loud, but my phone starts to ring again.

"The same guy?" Derek asks.

"It better not be."

I pick up my phone and check the screen. The name 'Lyndsay' appears. Along with a red heart. I still have that red heart.

'It's her, isn't it?" Derek asks.

My sweaty finger hits the green button. I slowly bring the phone to my ear. "Hello?"

"Sorry, I meant to call your office phone. Anyway, I have a case for you."

"Oh."

The next few sentences she says freeze me to the core.

2

CHLOE'S FIRST INTERVIEW

C hloe wipes her eyes and blows her tiny delicate nose into a tissue. She can't look into the camera as I talk to her.

Yes. It's a video call. The world has stopped for us too. In certain cases we can get out the office, like for investigative work. But these casual interviews are mostly done on video call.

"I'm sorry we had to call you at this time, but."

Chloe manages a few moments of eye contact. "I just got an email and the picture. Then I phoned up. That's all. I've nothing else to show you."

The doorbell rings. No, not the actual doorbell. The fake one on the video call. The latecomer has just arrived.

"It's about time," I say.

Derek joins the video call. Chloe's eyes drop down to the floor again. And for some reason she doesn't lift them even for a single second while Derek is in the chat.

"What took you so long?" I ask.

"Had problems with the link."

That's just a polite way of saying I got out of bed late.

"Can't you tell this girl's upset, go get a glass of water!" I order Derek.

Derek seems lost. "Uh..."

"Uh... what?"

"I can't."

"What do you mean you can't?"

I realise. I've gone mad.

What else could I have said to Derek? I got so used to having meetings in the police station and making sure there's always a glass of water at the table. This 'virtual' world is alien to me. No shaking hands. No asking for water, or food. It's weird.

I have to save myself in front of Derek and Chloe. I can't embarrass myself, no way. "I mean YOU should go get a glass of water for yourself, Derek. You're going to ask Chloe a few questions, better you have water with you in case. Your mouth. Gets. Uh, dry."

I clear my throat. Not that it will magically force them to forget the past two minutes, but anyway.

"Chloe, this is Derek, he'll be asking you a few questions along with me."

"But why?" Chloe asks. "I told you, I don't have anything else."

"Okay," I say. "But you and your friend, Max, were the last ones to be in contact with, what's her name again?"

"Anisa."

"Yeah, her. Uh... you were the last two people who spoke to her before she, uh, she..."

"Got murdered," Derek interrupts.

"We don't know that yet."

"Then why didn't you say that?"

"I was about to, but uh-"

"Wait a second. How would you know if me and Max were the last two people who spoke to her?" asks Chloe.

"Well, we don't know for sure, but that's what this post suggests, which An-" My mouth stutters. It never stutters when saying someone's name.

"Anisa," whispers Derek.

I can't risk embarrassing myself by trying to repeat after Derek, so I move on. I open a social media post on my computer. "This was the last post, she, sent, about your virtual Christmas party."

Chloe giggles slightly, like she's in disbelief.

"Why is that so funny?" I can't help but ask.

"Sorry, it's just that, Anisa never used to post anything. Sometimes, she would comment or like a post that me or Max put up, or a video on our channel."

Derek finally remembers he can ask questions too. "You have a channel?"

"Yeah, we upload our sketches on it. And I would sometimes upload the odd monologue. Um... what does the post say, by the way?"

I zoom into the post I opened before, and read it aloud. "The post was sent on the 2nd December, 12:23 pm. It says, 'Can't wait for my virtual Christmas party with Chloe and Max this evening. Been fed up, stuck alone in my flat. Finally got something to look forward to.' Smiley face. Love heart. Then, another, smiley, face."

Silence. Chloe tries to process.

"Anything else?" she asks.

I look past those silly, what are they called, emojis (did I not mention I'm in my 40s?), and I check to see if there's anything else.

Nothing. "That's about it. Then the day after that, the 3rd December, was when we got a call from our colleague Lyndsay. She said you phoned up about An-" That stutter again.

"Anisa," Derek completes.

Okay, I've had enough. "Just, you, carry on, please," I say to Derek.

"Um. Okay, uh. Okay, so you phoned up, panicking about the picture you got of Anisa. You sent the picture and Anisa's address to Lyndsay. A few officers went to the flat, and. They found her on the chair. And, yeah, she was. Dead."

That last word makes my body shiver. The word is all too common in my line of work, but for some reason, it feels new today.

"Okay," I say. "Back to the post. She said, very clearly, 'Can't wait for my virtual Christmas party with Chloe and Max THIS EVENING.' Then the next morning, you got the email and the picture. So, between your virtual Christmas party and her..."

"Her death," Derek kindly finishes for me, like it's becoming his job now.

"Her, death, it was unlikely she had been in contact with anyone. And, she said, 'Been fed up, stuck alone in my flat.' Which suggested that she hadn't been in contact with anyone, or had any visits, for a long time. And she lived alone as well, am I right?"

"Yeah," Chloe replies. "You're right, but, what are you trying to say, that me and Max have something to do with-"

"No no no, we just know so far that you and Max were her most closest contacts, and, most recent. So, if there was anything odd, anything she said or did in the Christmas do or at any time leading up to that event that you and Max noticed, please. Let us know."

"Everything was fine," Chloe says. "Anisa was normal, there was nothing strange or different about her recently."

"How was the Christmas dinner, you had loads of fun, yeah?" Derek asks.

"It was fine."

Chloe takes us back to the day of the virtual Christmas do. To the goofy jumpers she, Max and Anisa were wearing. To the laughing and joking around on screen. To the dinner they ate in front of the camera.

"We were getting along great," Chloe says. "We laughed, we chatted for hours. There was nothing weird about Anisa."

"What about before the dinner?" I ask. "You had any meetings then with her, was there anything different?"

"No, nothing." Her eyes water once again. "Please, can you ask me questions some other time, it's only been a couple days."

Derek and I look at each other. And we're both thinking the same thing (I hope).

That we're not going to get anything more out of her. Not today anyway.

***

Chloe's porcelain skin turns red in rage. "Out of all the times she could have posted something in her life, she had to do it the day before she-"

"You're, uh, acting like she knew what was going to happen the day, uh, after," Max stutters.

"Okay, it's just, I don't know..."

"Look, it's only a, uh, post. Nothing else. Just stay, uh, calm. We have nothing to, uh, hide."

"Yes you do. WE do."

"We, uh, do?"

"Yes, we uh uh do," Chloe mocks. "That officer was there."

"HE was, uh, there?" Max asks.

"Yeah, HE. I don't think he recognised me, but still."

***

Derek's an idiot for wearing sunglasses in our video call. First of all, we're INDOORS. Second, they're not even REAL! He has one of those silly filters on.

"Forensics team said there were no stab wounds on the body. But poisoning, that's possible. I had a quick look round Anisa's flat after," he tells me.

"Can you take that bloody filter off, I can't take you seriously with those bloody black blobs staring at me!" Not that removing the filter will make me take him more seriously, but anyway.

"No it's cool," he says. I think we're at that stage now in our work life where no matter how much I yell at him, he'll do whatever he feels like because he feels comfortable around me. Which is good, and also bad. At this moment, bad.

"Right, so, where was I? Oh yeah, I went to look around the flat for clues. They took her body away for tests. Which was good for me cos, you know, dead bodies. Eww. I messaged you to come, but you didn't answer me."

Then I remember. He did email me. My habit is always to reply to emails straight away before they pile up in my inbox. But this time I didn't. "Oh, yes. I remember. Sorry, I was busy with other things."

"That's okay," he replies. "I took some pics. I even sent them to you."

There's the second email I didn't reply to. "You sent me pictures?"

"Yeah mate, what's wrong, you don't wanna help me out in this-"

"I'll do my bit, alright? I don't slack off like you. And at least I showed up at the meeting on time."

"I was late because-"

"Because you had problems with the link. Okay." I still think he got out of bed late.

3

CHLOE'S NEXT INTERVIEW (WITHOUT ME)

S o I'm off for a week. Yes, Christmas is just round the corner, but still. I need time away from this case. Don't ask me why.

To be honest, I feel a bit sorry for Derek having to do all the interviews, but at the same time, I just can't get myself to open that wretched laptop. Forget the laptop, I'm struggling to even get out of bed.

It's not like me. I love work. I love keeping busy. But there's something about this case. It's pulling me away from the screen.

And towards a dusty box of tablets on my bedside table.

***

Derek scurries his mouse all over the computer screen.

At the other end, Chloe rolls her eyes, arms crossed. It's her second video interview.

"Is the other guy not joining?" she asks.

"Gordon? No, he's off for the week. I'm just trying to find... oh, there it is."

He clicks on what he was looking for.

His beloved sunglasses filter.

"How do I look?" he asks Chloe.

Chloe performs her signature eye-roll. "Can you just skip to the part where you ask me pointless questions so I can then leave?"

"Look, I know it's not fun for you, but we have to chat with you and Max a little more."

"I told you the last time, I never noticed anything strange about Anisa. And everything went fine during the Christmas do."

"You must have had some tiffs with her in the past. All friends do." By the way Derek still has the filter on.

"No, not really. She was never the kind of person who would get into an argument."

"What about Max?" Did you get along with him?"

"Yeah, yeah," replies Chloe, her pitch slightly higher than usual.

"Can you go back and remember if you had any conversations with Max about Anisa in the lead-up to her death?"

"Conversations about Anisa?"

"Yes, any conversation. No matter how small."

Chloe's mind runs through every word, every sound, every second of that fateful day.

The awful sketch rehearsal with Max.

Him saying goodbye and leaving the meeting.

The PING of the email notification.

"Anisa?"

Chloe grows uneasy as she pictures Anisa in her chair.

And then that SCREAM.

"What's on your mind?" Derek asks.

"Nothing, um. What were you asking again?"

"You and Max. Did you chat about Anisa recently?"

"Uh... no, not really. We never chatted alone for a while about anything, since..."

"Since when?"

"Since way back. I'm talking months and months..."

***

This is another sketch rehearsal between Chloe and Max, months ago. At least, according to Chloe.

Chloe delivers her lines, word for word. And so does Max- except with the added 'uhs' and 'ums'.

Though this time, Chloe has enough- "Would you stop it with the uh uh uh, you're doing my head in!"

"I'm saying my, uh, lines properly."

Chloe groans.

"I thought it was, uh, going great," Max stutters.

"Only because you're deaf in one ear."

"No I'm, uh, not."

***

Chloe and Max's bickering fades into the background.

"So we quit working together," Chloe explains to Derek. "And we haven't uploaded any new sketches to our channel."

"Okay," Derek says. "And you haven't spoken much to him since then?"

"Only time was really when we had the Christmas do. And that was about it."

"Alright. That's fine, I think it's about time I have a chat with Max. Thanks for joining today."

"I could say 'no problem', but I'd be lying."

"It's good to be honest. It's good to be you. I'm me. See?"

Chloe stares at Derek's virtual sunglasses, which end up on his nose.

"Oops, don't know how it got there. Anyway, it's good to be ourselves. So thanks for doing that. I'll just let you go now..."

As Derek's about to end the video call, a question springs to mind-

"Sorry, I've been meaning to ask..." His glasses stupidly slip down to his lips. "Have we met before?"

Chloe freezes. Derek's face is something to laugh at, but she can't.

"Uh... no," she replies.

"Oh. I thought, you looked familiar. Or maybe you just have one of those faces, I don't know."

"Maybe." Chloe looks like one of those typical wannabe actresses that have perfect skin, dancing hair, and a bit too much confidence for their ability. Except this is one of those rare occasions where Chloe actually has a touch of nerves.

"Right, take care," Derek says, before he and his sunglasses disappear from the video chat.

4

DEREK ACTUALLY DOES SOME WORK

Derek's in serious work mode.

The fact that he has his 'geeky mad scientist' glasses filter on proves it.

He studies through each picture he took in Anisa's flat. The half-drunk glass of juice. The half-eaten plate of food which appears to be some sort of roast chicken with vegetables and gravy.

He stops at a picture of a piece of paper. Dated 2nd December.

A range of letters and numbers are scattered across the page like so:

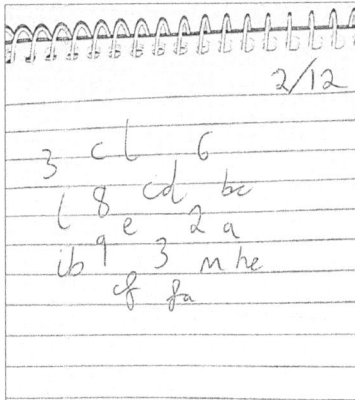

Derek types up an email:

Hi Gordon,

Thought I'd send you these, case you missed them. Again.

Please have a look.

Half-eaten meal and half-drunk glass. Interesting, right? Will wait and see if anything shows up in the toxicology reports.

The paper clue seems very intriguing. Challenge you to solve it.

Regards,
Derek.

Derek hits 'SEND'.

***

It's my first day back to work.

The past week flew by. And not in a good way.

You know when people say, 'time flies when you're having fun'? That wasn't true for me.

Time was flying while I was doing absolutely NOTHING. I spent most mornings in bed. That wasn't normal. I would always get up 7am SHARP.

I only just learned what a snooze button was.

You know when someone is bored, they're just dying for the hands of the clock to turn quickly. I wasn't like that. I was dying for time to stop. I didn't want Monday to ever come.

But it did. Here I am, sitting at my desk, staring at the computer screen, not wanting to touch the mouse. Time is 8:17am.

An email notification suddenly pops up.

I don't want to lift a finger today, but I have to. I open my inbox. An email from Derek.

I have a quick skim through the text. Notice the photo attachments. Hover the cursor over them.

But I don't open any.

I run out of my inbox. Turn the screen OFF.

No more today.

5

DEREK AND I CATCH UP

Max huffs like a spoilt little kid.

"I had to delete those videos, okay?" explains Chloe on video chat.

"But they were getting so many, uh, views."

"We can upload them again later. For now, the channel has to be clear of videos from that date."

"I can't go through so much time without uploading any, uh, sketch," Max moans.

"Relax, no one is desperately waiting to watch a video of you saying 'uh uh uh'."

"At least my acting's better than, uh, yours."

Chloe's LIVID. Her anger somehow magically flushes out an instant bushy moustache above her red lips. A bushy, BLACK moustache. Not so pretty with the red lips and blonde locks.

"Hey, uh, Chloe, when was the last time you, uh, shaved?" Max asks.

"I don't shave my face you dunce! What is going on?"

Chloe panics, her mouse racing all over her computer screen. "How do you get rid of this?!"

"Uh, you, uh…"

"Who am I even asking?"

The filter strangely disappears on its own.

"You, uh, figured it out?" Max asks.

"No, I. It just, went away by itself. Anyway, let's just move on."

***

"I tried so hard to make you happy. Even when my friends kept telling me to leave you."

Chloe stares into the camera.

"That you're not worth it. But I didn't listen to them. I thought maybe they were jealous. But I was wrong."

She tears up.

"I was so stupid. I thought I had to change myself for you, but the truth is. You were the one who had to change."

Her acting could do with a bit of work.

Yes. It's acting. Only a clown talks like this in real life.

Derek tortures me by sharing his screen on video call and playing one of Chloe's famous monologues.

"Why are we watching this?" I can't help but ask.

"I thought it might help," Derek replies.

"With what?"

"With getting to know more about her."

I let out a big sigh. Dying for the holidays to come sooner.

Chloe looks like she's reaching the climax of her dramatic monologue as she SCREAMS at the camera.

"Which play is this from?" I ask.

"I don't know," Derek says.

I'm one of those 40-something men who can't understand the appeal of social media. Sure, it's useful sometimes. Like for this case. But other than that, I just don't get why people are so interested in this RUBBISH. I don't get why people have the urge to post a picture of the avocado toast they ate this morning. I couldn't care less if they had avocado toast or a tall pile of bloody pancakes.

People only see what you want them to see. They see you holidaying in the blimmin' Bahamas, with your perfect face shaded underneath a sun-hat, the ocean washing up on the sand behind you. But what they don't see is the rest of your body drenched in red from sunburn, before being drowned in layers upon layers of sunscreen to prevent sunburn which is bloody POINTLESS because the sunburn has ALREADY happened.

Anyway, I've had just about enough of this monologue. "Can you turn it off please." PLEASE.

Derek reluctantly stops the video and exits the screen share.

"Have you seen the email yet?" he asks.

"Uh... yes." I'm not lying, technically.

"So... what do you think?"

"Well. Until we get the toxicology results we won't know if there was any poison in the drink or the meal."

"And the meal looked like something you would eat for Christmas dinner."

"You mean, roast turkey?"

"Could be. Was hard to tell. It could have been roast pork or-"

"No, she didn't eat pork," I interrupt.

Derek falls silent. Stares at me.

"How do you know?" he asks.

"Know what?"

"That she didn't eat pork."

"Because, uh." My lips are trembling. "Because, she was Muslim, right? They don't eat pork. Or celebrate Christmas. But this Christmas do was something else."

"Okay," Derek says slowly, in the same tone of suspicion one would use with a potential culprit in the interrogation room.

"Um." I'm thinking how to shift his focus. "Did you ever see her body?"

"No I didn't. I never did."

"Oh."

"I'm thinking. Let's just assume that she got poisoned from something she ate or drank at the Christmas do. Then the next day, Chloe got the email with the picture, she called the police. Some of the officers went to Anisa's flat, pronounced her dead. But I didn't see the body, and you didn't see the body. You know what that means?"

Derek's a different man when in work mode. But sometimes, I really want him to act dumb and ask dumb things like what hand he's holding up. I'm missing that Derek very badly.

"You said the forensics team did a toxicology test on her, and we're waiting on the results," I say.

"Yeah, and?"

"And, I think while they were examining her they would have noticed if she was still ALIVE!"

"Oh." An awkward silence. "Sorry I went off at a bit of a tangent there."

That was that. "What do you think of the paper clue?" he then asks me.

"What paper clue?"

"Okay, you ignored my message or it went to spam. I don't know what's more hurtful, you skipping my message or you not adding me to your contact list man-"

"Just stop it!"

"Fine," he says. FINALLY he's got the message that I don't want to talk about this ANYMORE.

Before leaving the chat, he can't help to say one more thing- "By the way, there's this psychologist I know, Dr Angela Bleakely, she can maybe help you with managing your stress-"

"Bye, I'm leaving."

My finger reaches for the button, as Derek carries on, "She takes appointments virtually, in case you're interested-"

His sentence cuts short. I'm out. Finally.

I sigh with relief. Until my phone rings.

"Hello?"

A deep, skewed voice penetrates my ear. "You can't avoid those emails for long."

"What are you talking about, what emails? Who is this?"

They hang up. "Hello?" I say. No answer.

I check the number that called me. I can't recognise it.

I slap the phone down on the desk. I know I should call that number back, just to check.

But I don't. I open the not-so-dusty-anymore box on my bedside table. And pop another pill down my throat.

6

— ◦ —

MY OLD APPOINTMENT WITH ANGELA

M y office phone used to ring on repeat all day. It was music to my ears.

There was one particular time that it rang. Every afternoon, around 1pm, before I took the first munch into my sandwich.

"Hello?" I asked when I answered that call. With a grin.

"I need to report a missing person," a lady would reply.

"Yes ma'am, your relation to them?"

"Wife. I think he might be kidnapped."

"Kidnapped? By who?"

"By someone so evil, that even the sound of their name drills fear into every living human being who's walked this earth."

"Oh my goodness. What IS their name?"

"OFFICE."

She would crack all sorts of jokes at lunchtime. And it was always my office phone she rang. Why? Because she knew I barely answered my mobile during office hours.

Eventually, as time went on, even our call on the office phone had to get cut short because of annoying colleagues. "Gordon, can you have a look at this case file? Gordon, you got a minute? Gordon, I know you're on your break, but can you check the email I sent you? Gordon, someone important is going to call you in the next half-hour, so can you end the call you're on just now, please?"

And it got to her. I knew it. The jokes stopped. The laughing stopped. It was mostly just a "hello," "how are you?" and "what are you doing today?" We were talking to each other more like colleagues.

Which we were. She was in a different office, handling the admin side of things, human resources, whatever you call it. And I was looking through case files, doing all that Sherlock Holmes kind of stuff.

This was how I rattled on and on during sessions with my psychologist, Dr Angela Bleakely. Yes, that Dr Angela Bleakely Derek was recommending. I was already having appointments with her for some time.

And the lady I was talking to on my office phone. Lyndsay. Yep, that same Lyndsay from before. Wife. Correction, wanting to be ex-wife.

The only time she calls me now is every few weeks or so, in the evening. I would sit on my couch, laptop on my, well, lap. If I have time I would brush my hair and shave. And clothes, well, let's just say my office uniform was upgraded. To pyjamas.

"Didn't you wear that last time?" she would ask me on video call every time I wore that shirt with the sleeping emoji.

"You got it for me last year, remember?"

"Yeah, I remember. I'm surprised you remember."

"Course I remember these things. Please, Lyndsay, I-"

"No. I told you, I need a few months away. To think."

"Can't you think while staying here?"

"I'm not in the mood for jokes right now."

***

"Lockdown's made things worse. Lyndsay has a support bubble with her sister's family. She'd rather cuddle her annoying 2-year-old nephew than me."

"So you do miss that physical interaction you had with your wife?" Angela asked me on video call.

"No, I enjoy being alone at home all day and hugging my pillow, of course I miss interacting with her! Sorry, I." I sipped some water.

"It's okay. I'm sorry Gordon, these may sound like silly questions, but I just want to know what's going on inside your mind in this moment. Bear with me."

"Yeah, sure. I understand."

"Gordon, how do you feel about increasing your dose?"

"I don't know, I just think it won't make any difference. It helped me a little bit with sleep and appetite and all that, but it's not going to be a-"

"A miracle cure?"

"Yeah, that."

"No medicine is. But they do help with motivating you."

"Motivating me to do what? There's nothing to do! There are no new cases coming in, I'm bored to death in this flat-"

"Then find something to do. A hobby. What did you enjoy growing up?"

7

MAX'S FIRST INTERVIEW

"Hey Gordon, did you know that you can see your face and my face side by side?"

Derek plays around with the video call settings (as usual). He always finds something new to be amused about.

Right now he's screwed up the video call settings so much that my face doesn't even take up the full screen anymore. Not that I'm obsessed with how I look, but. Anyway, I got used to the speaker view setting where the person who speaks in a video meeting takes up the full screen.

But Derek has kindly messed everything up and we are now in gallery view. Which means that the screen is now 50:50 me and him. Don't like it.

"Can you fix it please, Derek?" I ask him.

"Why, this looks better." No, it doesn't.

"Derek?"

"Okay, fine."

Derek finally switches back to speaker view. Thank God he's done it in time. Max's interview is just a few minutes away.

***

"What happened during your virtual Christmas do with Anisa and Chloe?" Derek asks Max on video call, with his goofy sunglasses on again.

"Uh, did, Chloe not tell you?" Max asks.

"She did. Now you tell me."

"Uh, well..."

He takes us back to that day, towards the end of the party, where everyone started to wave goodbye. "It went fine, uh, nothing strange. Except the goofy Christmas jumpers we were, uh, wearing. But something did happen near the end, when we were saying, uh, goodbye."

"What was that?" Derek asks. By the way I'm here in this video call. I just can't be bothered with asking questions.

"I left the group chat, but then very soon I realised I didn't actually, uh, leave. All I did was turn my, uh, camera off, so I was hidden from the main screen. I tried to leave the chat properly but I, uh, noticed that Anisa and Chloe were still on. They were, uh, talking, Chloe especially. I couldn't remember what it was about, uh, exactly, but they looked a bit serious. And then, uh, all of a sudden, Anisa started coughing. Quite badly. Chloe looked, uh, worried. Anisa got a tissue from her desk, she, uh, coughed into it. Then she noticed, along with the rest of us, that the, uh, tissue was covered in blood. Chloe was so shocked she couldn't, uh, speak. For once. And Anisa, well, she was the most, uh, surprised. I was about to ask her if she was okay, but by then it was, uh, too late. In a panic, she left the group chat and we didn't hear from her, uh, again. Me and Chloe tried calling her so many times but, uh, she didn't answer. We thought about going to her flat, uh, just to make sure she was okay. Eventually she, uh, messaged us both, later that evening, saying she was fine and that there was nothing, uh, to worry about. Me and Chloe then met each other virtually, uh, the next day-"

"You two were in touch after the Christmas do?" asks Derek.

"Yeah, a little. We had to, uh, rehearse a new sketch. No wait, uh, no. We didn't. I was thinking back to, uh, a rehearsal we had many months ago, uh, sorry."

"Okay, so you didn't meet Chloe the next day?"

"Uh, no. I didn't. But she messaged me to say that she got some, uh, email. It was an unknown sender, but there was a, uh, a picture labelled 'Anisa' as an attachment. She opened the, uh, picture, and. You know."

"Okay. Chloe sent us the email address of the sender, maybe that will help us. Did she say anything else?"

"No, she was just, uh, worried. She called the police, then, uh, they went to Anisa's flat and, you know."

"Right. Can you maybe go back further, I mean, before the Christmas do. Was there any conversation you had with Anisa?"

Max thinks for a moment. He remembers something. "Yeah. Yeah, uh, a few weeks before that, Anisa invited me and Chloe to a group chat. We had no idea why. It felt, uh, a bit out of the blue. Usually, Anisa was never the one to, uh, set up meetings or anything. But this time she did, and she, uh, said to me and Chloe... 'I'm leaving'."

"Leaving?" Derek asks.

"Yeah, she meant, uh, she was leaving the city. For good. She didn't say where she was, uh, going, just that she needed a change in environment or something like that. And, uh, she was not going to invest in the channel anymore. Chloe didn't take the news very, uh, well. I tried to, uh, calm her down."

"I never saw Anisa in any of your old videos on the channel."

"Yeah, she was more, uh, behind-the-scenes. She wasn't into acting much. But when we became, uh, friends, she found out me and Chloe liked to do sketches and upload them online. We were using our, uh, phone cameras before and wanted to upgrade to proper, uh, recording equipment, but we were broke. Anisa said she had some, uh, spare cash, so she helped us get going. With getting the, uh, equipment set up, promoting the channel..."

"Was Chloe more upset about her leaving the channel, or leaving the city?"

"Both, really. But, uh, I tried to explain to Chloe that it's Anisa's choice and that we, uh, should just be happy for her. So we had this, uh, Christmas do. It was more of a, uh, leaving dinner really. We wanted to meet up in person, but we couldn't, you know. We haven't seen each other in, uh, ages. The closest I got to seeing Chloe was through the, uh, mulled wine she sent us."

"Mulled wine?"

"Yeah, Chloe and her family are obsessed with it this time of, uh, year. She would send me and Anisa a bottle every, uh, December. She never stopped this tradition, uh, even now."

Derek turns off his filter, and for the first time, starts taking notes of what Max is saying. Minus the constant and irritating 'uhs'.

8

THE MULLED WINE

Derek switches the video call to gallery view. Now I have to see his stupid face take up half the screen again.

"Are you joking me?"

"I didn't do anything," he says.

"Oh, so it magically changed by itself."

The setting returns to speaker view thankfully.

But switches back to gallery view AGAIN.

"Really?"

"I swear I'm not doing it."

Back to speaker view. One second, two seconds, three, four. Seems to be stable now.

"Right, I think it's fine," I say.

"Cool, should we talk about Max a bit now?"

"Yes please, if it stops you fiddling with the settings-"

"For the millionth time, it wasn't me. Anyway, whatever. About Max. The mulled wine is interesting. If we're thinking of Anisa being poisoned. And now there might be a motive, she left Chloe and Max. But it's still a very weak motive, I mean, who kills someone just because they stopped helping out with filming their silly sketches?"

"Also Anisa wouldn't have drank the wine."

"Yeah, true. The drink that was left half-drunk on her table was orange juice. Not alcoholic."

"Right, so, leave it for now. Until we get the toxicology report, why is it taking so long anyway?"

"Don't know. You tried solving the paper clue?" Derek asks.

"Huh? Uh, yeah yeah, I'll look at it."

"Why don't I just open it now-"

"I said I'll look at it!" I scream.

I don't know what has come over me. Derek just sits there, awkwardly quiet.

***

"I never sent her anything. Anisa never drank wine. Yeah, I would send it to Max every year."

Chloe faces another round of interviews.

Derek shares his screen with me and Chloe. Thankfully he got bored of the sunglasses filter now and looks normal for once.

He opens an image. It's the paper clue.

"I saw this on her table. Does it mean anything to you?" he asks Chloe.

Chloe looks closely at the paper, puzzled. "No, I've no idea what it is. Anisa liked to fiddle with a pen and paper during our video calls, so she maybe scribbled a few odd letters and numbers."

"It's dated. 2nd of December. The day you had your Christmas do."

"So? Maybe she scribbled that during the call, I don't know. I couldn't always see her hands on screen and know what they're doing."

Derek and I exchange a look. This is going nowhere.

***

"You idiot!" Chloe screams at Max.

"I couldn't help it, uh, sorry. It's not like you're in the, uh, video. It's just me acting."

"But you uploaded the video to OUR channel."

"Right, sorry. I'll, uh, take it down."

"Forget it. They might have already seen it, there's no point. And didn't I tell you to make our stories match?"

"What do you mean, they, uh, did," Max replies.

"The mulled wine? Anisa coughing? Her leaving the channel? Her leaving the city?"

"Didn't you tell them all that, uh, stuff?"

"No, the point is, the less you say, the less they will ask."

Chloe sighs. That eye-roll again.

"Why would you even mention that I send mulled wine every year? It's not relevant, you know I only ever send it to you, not Anisa."

"What are you talking about, you, uh, always sent it to her."

"No I never."

***

"I had another look round Anisa's flat, no sign of mulled wine any-where, not even in the rubbish bin. Maybe Chloe was right, she never sent it to her."

Derek's giving another one of his updates to me on video call.

"Or maybe she did send it and Anisa used it up quickly. I don't know," he goes on.

"Until we get the toxicology results there's no point even thinking about this," I say.

"But Chloe and Max, they're hiding something, I-"

"Give it a rest, will you?! This is not the only case going on at the moment."

"But it's like this is not even a case to you at all," Derek says.

I feel attacked. Insulted. By a guy who's obsessed with silly filters. Not that he's using them right now, but still. "What's that supposed to mean?"

"It means, you never looked at the pictures I sent you properly, whenever I bring it up and ask if you want us to look at it together, you make an excuse to leave."

"That paper is just scribbles! Chloe said it herself, that girl liked to fidget all the time."

"A very organised scribble if you ask me."

"You know what, if you're so sure that this paper means something and it's not just some random scribbles then why don't you solve it, huh? I have enough on my plate already."

"Your plate is empty."

That sentence is a humiliating blow to my ego. The AUDACITY. "Excuse me?"

"I had a chat with Lyndsay," Derek replies. "She said you're behind in logging your hours. And you're taking a lot of days off at short notice, even when we have the Christmas break coming up-"

"It's none of your business, okay?"

My face suddenly drenches in drag queen makeup. Derek bursts out laughing.

"Right, what are you up to?"

"It's not me," Derek says yet again.

"I can only expect this from an imbecile like yourself."

Derek giggles uncontrollably.

"It's not funny, turn the filter off right now!"

"I swear, I'm not doing anything."

The filter turns off by magic.

"See, it's gone by itself."

"Why is this happening?" I ask. "Is there a glitch or something?"

"Don't know. But if it makes you feel any better, you look great in drag."

If only my hands can phase through the monitor so I can strangle that guy.

"Okay, relax. The macho look suits you, sorry."

I notice a red light blinking in the top left corner of the screen.

"How long has that red light been there?" I ask Derek.

"From the start, I think."

"What does it mean?"

"It means the video call is, recording."

"WHAT?! You've been recording all this?!"

"No, I thought YOU were recording this meeting, I didn't press anything."

"I didn't press anything either. Oh my goodness, that drag queen filter-"

"Relax, no one will have a recording of this meeting."

"I swear, if I find out you've been recording this whole time and you send it to-"

"Who, Lyndsay?" Derek giggles.

"DEREK!!!"

9

STILL THE MULLED WINE

This meeting is between three people. Me, Derek, and Max. Yes, another interview. Derek can't help himself.

I let him take the reins as I sit in the back, bored, tired, dying to get off this carriage. "We had a chat with Chloe the other day about the mulled wine, she said she only ever sent it to you every December. Not Anisa. She said Anisa didn't drink."

"Yeah," Max replies. "You're right about the, uh, last part, she didn't use to drink, but you're wrong about the, uh, first part. Chloe sent her mulled wine every, uh, year. Me and her."

"But that doesn't make sense. You knew she didn't drink, Chloe knew she didn't drink. And she still used to send her the wine every year? What's the point sending something to someone every year that you know will never be used?"

"Well, maybe if you know that person will use it, uh, but in some other way?"

"What do you mean?"

"I mean, Anisa, she didn't drink, but, uh, she liked using wine for cooking. She would use the mulled wine in her, uh, sauce or something. I'm no chef really, but I do know how those sauces are, uh, made and it usually involves putting the wine in a, uh, heated pan. The alcohol gets burned off and you're left with just the, uh, lovely taste of the wine. You process alcohol to make vinegar, I know that. And everyone has vinegar, right? So how is, uh, processing alcohol to make a sauce any different?"

Funny that when this same topic was brought up with Chloe, her response was: "No, Anisa was very strict with that kind of stuff. She wouldn't use it for cooking even. I asked her why and she said that most of the alcohol would get burned off, but not all of it."

Max says in reply at his interview: "It does all get, uh, burned off. And if there's a tiny bit left, that'll never make you, uh, drunk. You'd have to drink, uh, tanks of the stuff to feel anything."

Chloe: "It was about principle. And how one thing can lead to another. You don't start smoking fifty cigarettes a day straight away. It always starts with one. You might hate it the first time, same with drink. But over time you get used to it. You start enjoying it. And then it becomes an addiction."

Max: "Anisa had a lot of, uh, self-control, she would use it for cooking and nothing else. If she was going to get hooked on drinking the pure thing, then, uh, how come I never saw her drunk at a party?"

Chloe: "Back in the olden days, when I used to invite her over for dinner parties, and I made lasagne, I had to make sure the white sauce I bought didn't have any white wine at all. That was how strict she was."

Max: "She was always flexible with these, uh, things. And by the way, doesn't lasagne have, uh, meat in it?"

Chloe: "It was vegetarian."

Max: "Chloe makes lasagne with, uh, mince."

Chloe: "She did eat meat. A certain type."

Max: "No, I don't think she used to eat-"

"THAT'S ENOUGH!" I interrupt. He's getting on my last nerve. And Chloe's answers annoyingly ring in my ears at the same time.

"Derek had another look round An-. The girl's flat, but there was no mulled wine anywhere."

"She probably, uh, finished it," Max says.

"Finished it?" asks Derek. "She must have made gallons of sauce if she used up the full bottle already."

"She maybe threw it away?" Max thinks. "It can go off, uh, pretty quickly if you don't store it properly."

***

Derek looks through Anisa's email account on his computer.

A few messages catch his attention.

Subject title- Virtual Filmfest- Thank you for registering! Subject title- Virtual Filmfest- 3 months to go till Early Bird Deadline! Subject title- Virtual Filmfest- Just 1 month to go till the Early Bird Deadline. Submit your masterpiece today!

Basically, all about Virtual Filmfest.

Which no one really heard of, so Derek searches online. Turns out it's a fairly new competition that started after the pandemic. With traditional film-making grounded to a halt, the Virtual Filmfest is all about breaking new ground and finding innovative ways to film movies. This competition is open to all kinds of film-makers, new and old, newbie and established. The films submitted need to have been made virtually with the actors. So, video call is an obvious option.

"Was Anisa planning on making a movie with you and Max?" Derek asks Chloe in a video interview later.

"Uh..."

"I looked through her account and found a lot of emails from Virtual Filmfest, you ever heard of that?"

"Um, yeah. Anisa sounded like she wanted to do a film with us and submit to that contest. But before we had the time to get a script together, she..." Chloe tears up slightly.

"The deadline is very close, she must have had some plan. Some script outline, anything."

"No, she had nothing."

"You sure?"

"Yes, I'm sure."

"And you sure Anisa didn't drink?"

"I never sent the wine to her in the first place, how many times do I have to tell you?! And if I did send her the bottle, which I didn't, and she drank it or cooked with it or whatever, then why would she have used it all up when Christmas was still weeks away?"

"She celebrated Christmas?"

"No, never celebrated it, but she still got involved with things. Otherwise we wouldn't have had our Christmas do."

Derek falls silent for a moment.

"Look, I have no idea what kind of theories you are coming up with, that I poisoned her or something, but just wait till you get the results in. Please."

Derek's silence lives a short life sadly: "Anisa was leaving you and Max for good. And she was not going to invest in the channel anymore. Right? Max told us. What I don't understand is, why you never mentioned it."

"Because it's not important."

"So you at least admit that it's true."

"Yeah, but. So what if it's true? It has nothing to do with this case. And why are you even paying attention to a guy who says 'uh uh' all the time?"

"That reminds me. I saw the video he uploaded the other day. I thought he was quite good."

"I would have done better."

"Oh. You knew that he uploaded a video to the channel recently. Even when you said you broke up."

"Uh, well, uh, I-"

"Looks like you picked up his habit."

"No I haven't. He, uh, he says it more than I do. Way more than I do. It's annoying. His acting's not half-bad, that's how I was friends with him and worked with him this long. But now it's over. Done."

"You're done with him. Important. Anisa was done with you and Max. Not important, right?"

"Uh..."

10

—∷—

THE PAPER CLUE AND MYSTERY CALLER

"One of them is lying," Derek goes on in our private video chat. The filter he has on today is the one where your head is too big for your body. It's so hard to listen to him while keeping a straight face. "About the mulled wine. And Chloe seems to care a lot about proving she and Max no longer do sketches together. Which is weird to me. And interesting."

Derek pauses. His oversized brain thinks for a moment. "I can have another look round Anisa's flat to see if I can find anything else, but I've been there a few times and I just feel that even if there is something else, I'll just end up overlooking it."

Derek pauses even longer this time. He stares at me. With his en-larged stupid face. And asks, "Would you mind having a look?"

"Me?"

"Yeah. Mate, maybe that's what you need, to get out of the house. It might help ease your stress."

"I'm not stressed."

"Okay, even if that's true, you should still go. We need a fresh pair of eyes to look at the place. I just think that I'm missing something."

"What's the point, we don't even know if she was poisoned-"

"If she was, then there's something there that will tell us how. And if she wasn't... then there still will be something there that will tell us how she got murdered."

"Why do you always think that it's murder? You could be over-complicating this."

"What do you mean? You think she... killed herself?"

"I don't mean anything. I'm just saying that there's no point trying to jump to conclusions yet. Anyway, I'm tired mate. It's five, I'm heading off. I'll speak to you tomorrow."

I leave the chat without saying goodbye.

***

Anisa's voice, her laughs, her chats. They painfully echo in my ears.

I try to work out the paper clue on my computer. While fatigued, stuffed and starved of sleep.

I pull out my special blue pen, hoping it might motivate me. I circle some letters, the ones that are not joined with other letters:

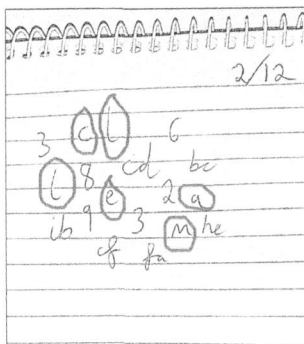

They look so random!

C, L, L, E, A, M

Maybe I have to rearrange them. 'MELLCA'? Wait, is that even a word? Sounds like a place. No, I'm thinking of Mallorca. One of those islands in Spain. I remember going there once, when travelling on a plane wasn't a crime.

But no, can't be that.

'CAMELL'? No, that's not how you spell it.

Wait. I got it. It's TWO words.

'CALL ME'. Makes more sense. I think.

Except who do I call? And how do I call them?

I explore the other letters in the clue. The pairs of letters joined together.

The f's are written strangely. Like fancy ribbons. Takes me back:

"Your 'f's are so weird, I can never make out what they are."

"They are 'f's, you just said that yourself."

"Only because you told me, otherwise I'd never know."

"You know now."

"Yeah, but what if you have to write to someone and they can't make out the words?"

"I only write by hand for myself. You wanted to read this so badly, I had to give it to you. Otherwise it was just for me."

I wipe my eyes.

My phone rings. I guess it's the world's way of saying I've done enough work today.

I close the picture and answer the call.

"Hello?"

"You're too afraid to go to her house?" There's that creepy, skewed voice again.

"You?"

"Yes, me. Why are you afraid?"

"Of what?"

"Of going to her house."

"Whose house?"

"Anisa's."

"Um. I, I don't know who that is."

"Such a wonderful human being you are. You become good friends with someone, then you say you never heard of them."

"It's none of your business. And what about you? What are you doing, hiding behind that creepy voice?"

"I don't have much to hide. But it seems as though you are trying your best to hide everything that you possibly can... Gordon."

My heart beats relentlessly, pumping sweat out of my skin.

"Hello? Hello?"

The mystery caller leaves.

11

—·—

CHLOE'S NEXT NEXT (NEXT NEXT) INTERVIEW

Derek studies Chloe for a moment. His filter today- a policeman's hat. "I know I asked this before, but I'll ask it again. And maybe you can tell me the truth this time."

"Ask what?" Chloe says.

"Do I know you from somewhere?"

Chloe freezes.

"You could at least act like you're relaxed, but no. It's written all over your face, that you're hiding something."

Chloe's acting fails her this time.

"You know what, I'm gonna play good cop today," continues Derek. "I'm gonna play good cop by letting you choose what you want to share with me. It could be, something about Anisa, or, something about yourself."

"There's nothing to share. About me."

"Then why do I feel like I've seen you before?"

"I don't know, it's just all in your head. And you creep me out whenever you say these things. I've never met you before. Ever."

"Okay, fine. Let's leave that for now. But what about Anisa?"

"I didn't do anything, she was my friend, why would I-"

"I'm not saying you did anything. Just tell me what you know about her that we don't already."

Chloe's eyes water. "Me and Max told you everything."

"Think harder. Please."

Chloe firmly shuts her eyes. She massages the sides of her forehead, as if that can somehow stimulate her mind.

"Come on," Derek says.

Chloe thinks as hard as her delicate little brain can let her.

Her eyes open wide. Fingers drop. Gloss-painted lips mouth the words...

"Writing group."

"Huh?" Derek asks.

"She joined a writing group over a year ago. I remember, she mentioned it sometimes. She sounded like she was enjoying it. But then."

"Then what?"

"Then, she stopped talking about it. Whenever me or Max brought it up, she tried to change to another subject. Then eventually, we stopped bringing it up altogether."

"So you never tried to figure out why she avoided the topic?"

"No, because I didn't see it as a big deal. I just thought, she wasn't enjoying it as much as she used to, that's why she didn't like talking about it anymore. And maybe she left the group. I don't know."

"You felt she was changing?"

"I don't know. I had no idea what was going on in her head. And then, out of nowhere, she said she was leaving us."

"What did she used to say about the club? What kind of stuff did she do?"

"Probably something boring, otherwise I'd remember. But I do remember the name of the group."

"What's the name?"

"'Write to Happiness'. Write as in 'w', 'r', 'i', 't', 'e', not the other right."

"Okay, got it."

"That's all I know. Or remember."

"It will do for now," Derek says, relieved to squeeze something out of her. "Thanks."

***

Derek's hard at work on his computer through the night. No sunglasses filter. No policeman hat filter. No big head and small body filter.

Just Derek with his no-nonsense strict work mode filter.

He researches the web page for 'Write to Happiness'. Pulls out his phone, and dials the contact number shown at the bottom.

No answer.

He looks at the time. No wonder there's no answer.

It's 3 AM.

As the dark hours of this long winter night draw to a close, Derek tries again to call the number.

He finally gets a response.

Derek flips open his notepad, and jots down a few things. As if they are names being given to him on the phone.

As his pen touches the page for the next name, he freezes.

12

---·---

THE TOXICOLOGY REPORT (AND MY BIG SECRET)

> The toxicology results finally arrive.
>
> The report confirms that NO POISONOUS SUBSTANCE was found in Anisa's body, or in the half-finished meal and drink on her desk.
>
> It is concluded that the CAUSE OF DEATH WAS NOT POISONING.

***

Me and Derek have another one of those awkward silences you usually get in video calls.

Except this one is not only awkward, but also depressing.

"Don't beat yourself up about it," Derek says. "It happens. This will be another one of those case files that will gather dust on the shelf. Well not literally. We're more eco-friendly now, we don't use much paper anymore."

I hear the ping of an email entering my inbox. I open the message.

"What is it?" asks Derek.

"Some meeting invitation," I reply. "From you."

"Me?"

"Yeah, it's your email address, derek.-"

"Mine is just 'd' then a dot. It's probably a scam."

"There's a link at the bottom," I notice.

"Better you don't click on it. Don't know where that'll take you."

I close my inbox.

"I know you don't like me asking this, but any progress on the paper clue?" Derek asks. Once again.

I don't know what to do. Should I tell him I got the words 'call me' so far? Maybe it's to do with the meeting link I got just now. But he doesn't want me to click on it for some reason. And the email address is similar to his.

I decide to say, "Chloe's right. It's just a bunch of random letters and numbers."

"Speaking of letters, and words..."

Derek searches something on his screen.

"I had a chat with Chloe the other day," he continues. "She mentioned that last year, Anisa joined some writing club."

"Why does that mean anything?" I ask.

"That's what I wanted to find out. The club was called, 'Write to Happiness'. You ever heard of it?"

"No, you mad? Do I look like someone who would join some lame writing club?"

"That's strange, because, I phoned them up and asked about who their members are, and were. Obviously, they didn't want to tell me the first try, but once I told them that it was part of a police case, they started co-operating. And there was one name they gave, that really surprised me, you know. You want to guess what that name is?"

"What's the name?" I ask.

Derek takes his time.

And mouths the name...

"GORDON FINDLATER."

My face freezes to ice.

The lips defrost enough to speak. "Uh... There must be other Gordon Findlaters around."

"You sure, cos I asked them if I could get more information so I could, you know, rule you out. But everything they gave me. Age, profession, place of birth. All points to you."

I can't face the camera.

"And let's face it, you're the only person in the world who has the name Gordon Findlater."

"Not true, it's quite a common surname," I argue.

"Come on mate, stop playing with me now," Derek says. "Why didn't you tell me? There's no shame in joining a writing club, I'm not judging you."

I sigh.

Derek's not going to let me go until I tell him my story...

***

"Motivating me to do what? There's nothing to do! There are no new cases coming in, I'm bored to death in this flat-"

"Then find something to do. A hobby. What did you enjoy growing up?"

That was the worst and best session I had with Angela. I couldn't wait around for work to come. And I couldn't sit around and do nothing. A hobby sounded like a good idea.

I liked writing since when I was a kid. I liked reading those detective books and I was coming up with my own stories, my own murder mysteries. But Angela's idea was not only for me to start writing again, but to do it with other people. So she recommended a writing club.

Write to Happiness.

It went virtual by the time I joined. That was where I met Anisa. We got along very well. Became friends, even. We were mostly writing short stories and poems when we were in the club but Anisa, in the background she was also writing a feature film script.

She told me about it later on. She was a bit shy about it, especially when I asked her if I could read it. Eventually she sent the script to me, it was hand-written at the time, she always did that with her first drafts. Obviously she kept the original and sent me a scanned copy of the hand-written script.

She told me that she was just writing this for fun and she wasn't serious about getting it further from the page. Anyway, I had a look through it, and I thought it was great. Anisa found that hard to believe. I encouraged her to go further and send it to a script contest. Or directly to an agent or producer. Most people never reply, but it was worth a try. She still wasn't sure about it. She was okay to leave the story on the page.

But I wasn't.

So I took matters into my own hands. I typed up her script and then sent it to a few production companies. No replies.

Then I sent it to some agents. Didn't hear back from any of them.

Except one.

It was an agent called Clive Wasserman. He said he normally never replied to unsolicited submissions, but he didn't have much work going on, given the way things were. And he was interested in the story so he read the first few pages, and eventually, the whole thing. He loved it.

We spoke on the phone soon after that, and he wanted to sign me up. I was about to tell him that the script wasn't mine and that I sent it on behalf of a friend who was too nervous to share it with anyone, but Clive, he was, showering me with praise.

He was so excited, that I was scared about telling the truth and letting him down. I was, enjoying getting that praise. It was something I never really experienced before, and I wanted it to carry on. But I didn't want to hurt Anisa. She was the one who did the work.

I plucked up the courage and told her what happened.

I tried to make her understand, but she couldn't. She was so upset. I felt terrible. All I wanted was to help her out.

That was the last time I spoke to her. I tried to call her many times after that, but she didn't answer. And even if I want to call her now and she wants to answer, she can't because...

***

"Gordon, there's so much you can do in this case," says Derek.

"I know, I know that if I get stuck in, I'll work it out, but. It's hard."

"I get it. But not doing anything will make things even harder. So what's worse? Hard, or harder?"

I manage a little grin.

And I think I know the first person who can help me...

13

ANGELA'S UNLIKELY INTERVIEW

"I have a case now, it's keeping me busy. In a good way."

"That's great," says Angela. This is a follow-up video call she had scheduled many months ago. "How about the writing?"

"Yeah, I'm taking a break for now, but I'll get back to it in a few months. Right now, this case is taking up a lot of my time."

"I understand. But remember what I said last time, you need to prioritise rest."

"Sure, but. Problem is, I won't get rest until I find out what happened to her."

"To who?"

"Anisa."

"Uh, um. Maybe we should reschedule this follow-up appointment-"

"Sorry, doctor. I can't reschedule. And this is not an appointment anymore. It's your interview."

"Gordon, I'm sorry, but I can't share personal information about other patients with you-"

"Informally, no. But if it's for gathering evidence in a suspected murder case, then yes."

"I didn't mean any harm, I was helping her, it broke my heart when I heard she passed away."

"I'm not saying you did anything to her, doctor. I just want you to tell me the whole story. If there's anyone who knows Anisa's deepest and darkest secrets, it's you."

"I'm not sure, this feels very strange-"

"Please."

Angela inhales and exhales deeply, like she's in a meditation class. "Okay."

"Great. Let me hit record first."

And that red light blinks on the screen...

"Anisa worked for an IT company for many years. Got overlooked for a promotion many times. Why didn't she leave? Job security, close to home, many reasons.

"She was very creative. She loved writing as a hobby. And she was into film, loved going to the cinema with her sister when she was younger. She wasn't like the typical girl who dreamed of being the lead actress in a major Hollywood blockbuster. She dreamed of being the person behind the scenes, coming up with the story, directing, all the hidden work. It sort of suited her character. She was creative, but shy. So working in the creative industry behind the scenes, sounded like the perfect career for her. But for now her 9 to 5 at the IT firm had to make do. And her family wanted her to have a 'normal job'.

"There wasn't much work going on in the office for a few months, so she decided to do some of her writing. Her colleague, Kylie her name was, she told on her. Poor Anisa got fired. She did nothing wrong, I mean there was no office work to do, so she was allowed to do whatever she wanted. Other people would waste time watching pointless reels or go on an online shopping spree, at least she was doing something productive.

"So Anisa lost her job, lockdown hit, she was stuck at home all day, and her parents were annoyed with her wanting to pursue her creative interests. You get all these ingredients, throw them together into a pot and in a few hours you're left with nothing but... an unappetising stew of depression.

"Some days were so bad she couldn't get out of bed. Family labelled it as laziness. And after a while she believed it.

"A couple of panic attacks later, she was referred by her doctor to a psychologist. Me. She was diagnosed with severe depression and anxiety. Family diagnosed her as a psycho who was possessed by an evil spirit, and they disowned her.

"Good thing was that Anisa had enough savings to be able to rent a place of her own and cover other expenses. She had regular sessions with me online, and she was prescribed with antidepressants for many months. It definitely helped in some way. The panic attacks were gone. But she felt empty. She needed to do something she enjoyed, and do it with other people.

"Then came along the club, Write to Happiness. It helped her get back to normal. She told me she made friends with someone called Gordon. I suspected it was you, but because of patient confidentiality, I had to, you know, keep quiet."

"And you did the same when I told you I made friends with someone called Anisa," I say.

"Yes. It was a secret I had to keep, for legal reasons. But I happily kept it. I was seeing two of my patients smiling, getting their life back. That was what really mattered to me."

"What about Chloe and Max? How did they show up?"

"Anisa came across their post where they were looking for someone to help with writing their sketches, directing, editing..."

"Behind-the-scenes stuff."

"Exactly. Anisa fit the bill. And the three of them became good friends. But then…"

"Then what?"

"Then after a while Anisa changed. Again. I had a check-up appointment with her and noticed her mood was off. I kept asking her what was wrong, but she wouldn't tell me. She just kept saying, 'no one likes me', 'everyone uses me', all these things. And that was the last I heard from her."

I sink back into my chair. "So you have no idea what happened from the moment her mood was off to the moment she was killed?"

"Yes, I'm afraid. I don't have anything else to share with you. But I hope that what I shared with you will help you in some way."

"There's something not right. I mean, from the story you gave me, it sounded like she was very distressed and tortured. And to top things off, she was murdered. I mean, it's like running over a deer that already has a broken leg. Who does something like that?"

"I don't know."

"Was she in contact with her family again?"

"No, they all shifted abroad when Anisa moved out. They don't even know she's dead."

14

ANISA AND CHLOE- AN OLD CHAT

"What's with all these comments?" Chloe complained in an old video chat with Anisa.

"Not everyone's gonna be a fan of your sketches."

"I know, but it's not about the sketches. They're... threats. Here, I'll share them with you." Chloe shared her screen with Anisa. "I disabled the comments just now but the ones that have been posted so far, we can see them when we sign into the account."

Anisa skimmed through the comments for one of the videos.

"You sign in as well, and look through them properly," Chloe continued. "See if there's any pattern."

Chloe stopped sharing the screen. "That's all. When you leave, you won't have to worry about this anymore, right? It'll just be me and Max dealing with it."

***

"I had a look through all the comments. They're mostly for certain sketches," Anisa told Chloe a few days later.

"Which ones?"

Anisa scrolled through her screen. "'Job interview gone wrong'. 'You owe me money'. 'Lockdown blues'. Do these sketches have anything in common?"

Chloe thought for a moment. And it hit her. "They were the sketches we were going to perform."

"Where? At that gig?" asked Anisa.

"Yeah. Remember, me and Max, at the start of the gig, we told the audience which sketches we were going to do from our channel. And those were the top three most viewed."

"So, the people who posted these comments, these threats even, they're anonymous, but we know now that they were in that audience."

"Yeah."

"That narrows it down."

"Not by much."

***

Derek flicks through his papers, his no-nonsense serious work mode filter on. Basically means, no filter on. Chloe sits nervously at the other end of the video call.

A previous conversation she had with Anisa runs in her mind:

"We all ran off by the time the officers came, except that one guy, he saw my face for a split-second. But anyway, we got away with it, so I don't know why they're even posting these comments."

"They've got nothing better to do, okay? And if they really wanted to scare you and tell the police what happened, they would have ended up in trouble as well. Just relax. It'll be fine."

Derek looks at the screen and begins his round of questions:

"You had these threats coming in and you and Max never told me? You should have reported it on the site, at least."

"It was nothing," says Chloe. "We get them all the time. And those comments were hidden, how could you have even found them?"

"Because, when I searched through Anisa's flat, I found a notepad which had a list of usernames and passwords for different accounts. One of them was for this website where you upload your sketches. You knew she had access to this account, right?"

"Uh, yeah, yeah. Me, Max, Anisa. We all had the account details so we could log in and do what we want."

"Like hide comments?"

"It's nothing. I don't know why you're focusing on something that's got nothing to do with Anisa and what happened to her. Shouldn't you check that writing club I mentioned the other day?"

"I am checking it out, don't worry."

Chloe nods gently. The sound of previous conversations with Anisa resume in her ears:

"I need the money back by end of this month. The new flat I'm moving into, there's a deposit-"

"Wait a minute, Anisa. We haven't even sorted this out yet and you're asking for money?"

"The money was for setting up the live gig. Which I didn't want to do, but you made me. And it never even happened."

"It did. For a few minutes."

"Look, I'm sorry. But I already spoke to the landlord, and he wants the deposit by the end of the month."

"I don't have that kind of money lying around at the moment."

"Obviously not in cash. It must be in your account, give it to me through bank transfer."

"I don't have that kind of money in my account either."

These lines torment Chloe, but she can't help thinking about them. It's like not wanting to watch a horror movie, but watching it anyway and then losing sleep for a week.

"Something you want to share with me?" Derek asks Chloe.

"Huh? Uh, no. No," stutters Chloe. "Um, what was it you found out so far about that club?"

15

MYSTERY CALLER TORTURES ME

M y eyes shoot open, mouth gasps for air.

I wipe my damp forehead. Look around frantically, pick up the clock from my desk to check the time.

It is 12:05. Past midnight.

I slam the clock back onto the desk.

My phone starts to ring.

I pick it up, can't recognise the number. Answer anyway. "Hello?"

"Slept on your chair, did you? Hope your nightmare was not too distressing."

"You again? Wait... how do you know I-"

"You have a bad habit keeping your camera lens exposed all day long."

I reach for the camera, about to flip down the cover when-

"Before you finally cover it, let me talk to that miserable face one last time."

"I don't understand," I say. "My computer's not even on, wait. Oh. It's in sleep mode."

"Much like you were."

The mystery caller cackles.

"Right, tell me what's going on. How can you spy on me, and why do you call at weird times and talk in riddles then hang up, huh?"

"Don't worry, you will know very soon."

"I'll know what?"

"About everything. About what happened at the Christmas do. About what happened to Anisa."

"How can you know about any of this?"

"I have something to show you. Some video footage."

"Video footage?"

The mystery caller hangs up.

***

"So he's called you many times then?"

Derek's unto me.

"I don't know if it's a 'he', but yeah. How they have the video footage of the Christmas do, I have no idea. Unless… they were there."

"You mean, you think it's one of those three?" Derek asks.

"Maybe."

"Right. Well, it can't be Anisa, for obvious reasons. That just leaves Chloe and Max. Did it sound like one of them?"

"I don't know."

"Did you not record any of the conversations? We could have played with the audio."

"I already told you, he called me randomly on my mobile and with different numbers every time."

"Okay. If he calls you again, just let me know," Derek says.

16

— · —

SOLVING THE ANNOYING PAPER CLUE

It's another late night of me playing around with the remaining letters and numbers in the paper clue.

I circle the joined letters in red, and the numbers in yellow. The paper clue is now nice and colourful (unless you're reading this in black and white in which case it would be different shades of grey. But hopefully you can tell the shades apart!).

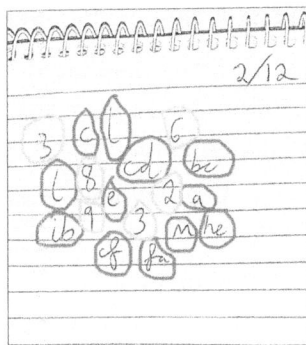

Right. So, the joined letters are 'cd', 'bc', 'ib', 'he', 'cf' and 'fa', if I'm making out the handwriting correctly.

And the numbers are '3', '6', '8', '9', '2' and '3'. Numbers are easier to make out, I have to say.

I stare at this kaleidoscope of letters and numbers for a long minute. And lose the will to live.

"Why don't you make any sense?!"

I collapse back against my chair, keeping my distance as far away from that infernal screen as possible.

But I can't give up. I have to keep going. It's the least I can do for Anisa.

So I lean forward again, and open the original image of the paper clue. Maybe looking at the original picture without all the colours and circles will trigger something in my brain.

5 minutes later. Nothing.

I close that picture, and return to the one I was scribbling on.

There must be some sort of pattern.

How many blue circles are there, 1, 2, 3, 4, 5, 6. Okay, 6. Red circles, also 6. Yellow circles, also 6.

So I know the blue circles are the ones that spell out 'CALL ME'. The red and yellow circles must be connected with each other and will tell me who the hell I'm meant to call, and how.

This has got to be one of those classic puzzles where you have to replace the numbers with letters. But there's already so many letters! Maybe it's the other way round? Those numbers '3', '6', '8', '9', '2' and '3' might be the numbers I need to call whoever the bloody hell I need to call.

Question is, what order do these numbers have to go?

That must be what those double letters are for.

Right, 'cd', 'bc', 'ib', 'he', 'cf' and 'fa' are the double letters. A is 1, B is 2, blah blah blah, so. These letters should become:

'34', '23', '92', '85', '36' and '61'.

And what are my single numbers again, '3', '6', '8', '9', '2' and '3'.

Time to stack them on top of each other:

```
   3    6    8    9    2  3
   34   23   92   85   36  61
```

Wait a second. These numbers show up in the double numbers! And the remaining numbers go from 1 to 6!

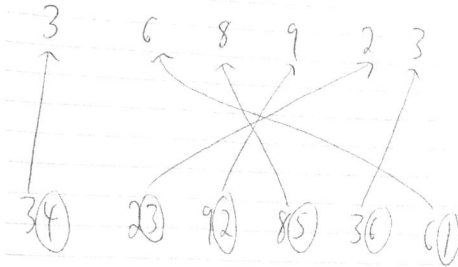

Right, all I need to do now is rearrange the numbers in order:

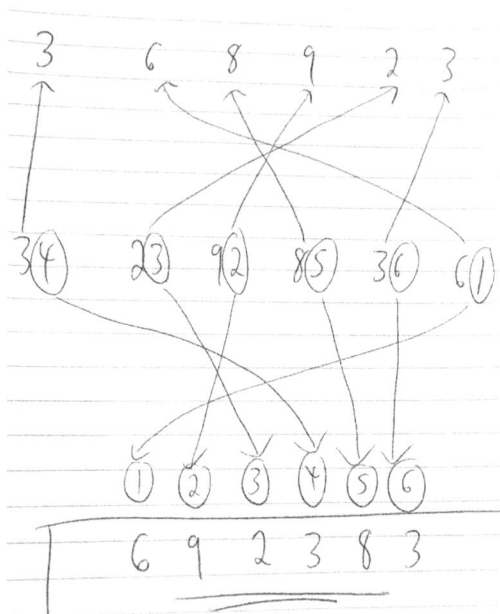

6 9 2 3 8 3

This is the number to call. Except how the hell do I call someone with just six digits!

Wait. If I add my area code before those six digits then it adds up.

I pull out my phone and dial the numbers. I press the phone to my ear, and wait.

No response. I try calling again, wait once more.

Still nothing.

I stamp the phone onto the desk, bury my face in my hands.

Wait. I remember something. How can I forget, I'm so stupid!

I rush to my computer and check my inbox for the email that I initially thought was sent by Derek.

I open that email, and see the link below for a video call. I click on it.

A box pops up, where I have to enter a password to join the video meeting. And guess what... it needs to be SIX DIGITS!

Might be a bit premature but I sigh in relief and type the six digits. I hit enter.

It's loading, loading...

I'm in!

I explore the meeting window and realise I'm the only one there.

I guess they didn't give a time, whoever they are. So I'll wait.

I lean back against the chair and glue my eyes to the screen. They become heavy, I drift off to sleep...

17

THE BIG SURPRISE

"GORDON?!"

My eyes explode open, mouth erupts into a shriek.

I can't believe what I'm seeing.

I rub my eyes. This can't be true.

"ANISA?"

There she is. In the video call. Staring at me.

"Is that really you? No, wait, it can't be you. I'm just seeing things."

"It is me," she says.

"What? No, no, I'm hearing things as well. Why am I hearing and seeing things that are not real? I'm dreaming, I must be dreaming."

I grab the glass of water from my desk. "I need to wake myself up."

I dip my fingers in the water, spray drops onto my face.

"I'm still here," she says.

"What? No, maybe I can..."

I pinch my arm. "Ow!"

She's still there!

I drench my entire face in water. Gasp for air like I had been plunged into a river.

The moment my eyes stop stinging I open them wide once more.

"Gordon it's ME, okay?!" she says.

"But how? You're meant to be. You're meant to be-"

"Dead?"

"Yeah."

"Well I'm not. I thought you'd never work out that paper clue."

"What paper clue? The paper, with the scribbles? And the-"

"The messy 'f's, yes."

"But, wait. I, I still don't get it, how, how can you be here, I don't understand. You were, you were meant to be dead. Chloe saw the picture, she phoned up the police, they went to your flat, they confirmed you were dead. It's, it just, doesn't make any sense."

"You weren't one of the other officers, were you? And neither was your sidekick."

"Who? Derek?"

"Who else?"

"But Derek, he went to your flat many times."

"He told you he never saw my body, right? Truth is, my body was never taken away by forensics. It was taken nowhere. It had two good legs that hopped over to another city while you were both working on the case."

"But why? Why did you have to go through all this?"

"Do I really need to answer that?"

I fall silent. Confusion makes way for guilt.

"Listen, Anisa. I'm sorry. I tried reaching out to you so many times, to say sorry. Again and again. I don't know, what more I can do. To make it up to you."

"Don't worry about it. You'll make up for things, without even knowing."

"Without even knowing? What does that mean?"

"You'll understand. But not today, some other time. Bye, Gordon."

"Anisa, wait!"

Anisa pauses reluctantly.

"I worked out the clue, didn't I? Took a while, but I got there in the end. Doesn't that show you enough that I care?"

"Did it really take you that much effort, or were you making up excuses before?"

"Not excuses, I swear I was just-"

"Scared? That seeing anything of mine would bring back memories? If you care about someone, you wouldn't want to forget them, would you?"

"I never forgot you." I draw out my box of tablets from the desk, and shove it into the camera. "Why you think I'm taking this, huh? I didn't need it for ages, that club helped me, but now. Now, I. I'm back to square one."

Anisa's hand reaches for the exit. "Me too."

***

Derek stares at me through the screen, like it's an interrogation.

"You sure it was her?" he asks.

"Yes, I'm sure. Why did she have an email address like yours?"

"I don't know, she's trying to mess with you. And I'm sure someone else is involved with her. It might be Chloe or Max, it might be someone else."

"Does it even matter? It's not like it's a murder case anymore that we have to care. It's just an, awful prank."

"An awful prank that wasted our time. Which does matter."

An email alert pops up on my computer.

"Who's that?" Derek asks.

"Don't know. I'll check." I open my inbox. "It's them."

"Who? That person who's been calling you?"

"Yeah. They sent the video footage."

"Well it's not going to be much good for the murder case since there isn't one, but it might help fill all these gaps."

"Or dig up new ones."

"Just play it already."

"Alright, alright."

As my cursor touches the play button...

"I want to see it too," Derek says.

"Okay, I'll share it."

18

THE VERDICT

I see four faces on today's video call. Chloe, playing with her fresh French manicure. Max, tapping his fingers away on his desk. Derek, without a filter (hooray). And me.

The clock reads 2:17pm. Meaning 17 minutes of awkward silences and fidgeting.

"Are we waiting on someone or what?" Chloe asks, fed up.

"Sort of," I reply.

"But we can make a start anyway, can't we?" Derek asks.

"I don't see why not. We've waited long enough."

"So what's this meeting for anyway?" Chloe asks. "You cracked the case or something?"

"Sort of," I say again.

"Are those the only two words we're gonna hear? 'Sort of'? Doesn't sound very convincing."

"No, we're convinced about a number of things, aren't we Derek?"

"Yep, we sure are," Derek says.

"Right. So, should we start from the beginning?"

We go right back to when we had that video call. Just me and Derek. Where he was holding up his right hand.

"Me and Derek were having, an important, video chat, when suddenly my phone rang. I thought it was gonna be one of those bloody cold-callers, but no. It was a colleague, Lyndsay.

"She got a call from you, Chloe, when you saw that picture of Anisa. You gave Anisa's address, a few officers went to her flat, and pronounced her dead.

"Me and Derek interviewed you a number of times to learn more about your relationship with Anisa.

"You blew your nose into a tissue. Might sound like a pointless comment, but I'll come back to it later. What interested me, and Derek, was the look on your face every time Derek was in the video chat. I know you act, but you did a terrible job at hiding your nerves there."

"What reason did I have to be nervous?" interrupts Chloe.

"That's where I can come in, Gordon," Derek says.

Chloe struggles to look towards the camera. Derek stares right at it with confidence:

"You and Max? Your little live performance that wasn't allowed to happen but you went ahead with it anyway?"

"W-what are you talking about?"

"Some months ago, me and a few other officers found out about this event that was going to happen. We couldn't let these big gatherings take place, so we turned up to disperse the crowd. But, when we got to the venue, everyone had pretty much ran off anyway. Including the performers. You, Max. And you, Chloe. I caught a glimpse of you, and I'm sure you saw me as well, otherwise you wouldn't have been so nervous in the interviews."

"This has got nothing to do with Anisa, I don't know why you're bringing it up."

"Actually, this story does tie in with Anisa a little bit. You made it clear in an interview that you and Max stopped doing sketches together. It was important to you that I believed this, for reasons I understand now. But soon after the interview, I saw that Max uploaded a video to your channel.

"I'm guessing you weren't very happy with him about that, but it was too late to take it down because you assumed I'd seen it already and it would look suspicious being removed. And you assumed right. I saw that video. Great delivery, but a bit too many 'uhs'."

"It's my, uh, style," interrupts Max.

"Right. Anyway, things were going so badly between you both, that you started making each other seem like the culprit with the whole mulled wine debacle."

"But, luckily for you both," I step in, "the toxicology reports came back negative, so we put that to rest. As for the gig..."

"Okay, I'll see if I have anything growing on my money tree to cover the fines," says Chloe. "Now if you excuse me-"

"Wait, we're not quite finished yet," Derek says. "Gordon, you want to move on to part two?"

"Part two?" I ask.

"Yeah, part two. The mystery caller."

"No, that's part three, part two is-"

"Oh yeah. The paper clue. Wait, that sort of ties in with the mystery caller."

"We can do both together if you want."

"Yeah, fine. Start it off."

"Okay," I say. "So, there were a few clues Derek picked up at Anisa's flat, which you're both aware of. One of them was a paper where Anisa scribbled some letters and numbers. Chloe, you said that Anisa was fidgety and that these were all random scribbles. But they weren't.

"I sorted them out and found that it was a meeting code. For a video call. I got a random email some weeks ago with a link to a video meeting. So I clicked that link and typed in the meeting code. It got me through. I waited, fell asleep even, then I woke up. And you know who I saw at the other end?"

Chloe half-cares as she asks, "Who?"

"It was..."

Suddenly we hear a doorbell in the video call. Beautiful music to my ears.

"The timing can't get any better than this," I say. "Switch your camera on, don't be shy."

The late VIP guest finally switches on their camera and waves.

Anisa.

"Anisa, you're alive?!" Max asks.

"Don't act so surprised," I say. "Anisa, you mind telling us what happened on the day of the Christmas do?"

"Sure," replies Anisa. "We had the party virtually, I coughed blood, left the call suddenly, it was all true. But after that..."

***

Anisa's doorbell rings. Her actual doorbell.

She opens the door.

Chloe and Max stand outside.

"What are you guys doing here, we're not in a social bubble," says Anisa, as she reluctantly invites the two into her living room.

"To hell with these social bubbles Anisa, we were worried sick about you," says Chloe.

"No you weren't. None of you care about me."

"If we didn't care about you, we wouldn't be here."

"Oh please, you just wanted an excuse to get out the house."

"And drive thirty miles to here?"

Anisa falls silent. Collapses to the couch, confused.

"We all care about you, uh, Anisa," stammers Max. "Are you feeling okay?"

"I'm fine."

"What about the, uh, blood?"

Anisa goes to her dustbin and plucks out a scrunched tissue. She opens it, revealing the stain of blood. "You mean this?" She throws it back. "It was ketchup. I know, I'm weird."

"Why would you pretend like this?" asks Chloe. "You wanted to check if we actually cared about you? Come on, Anisa."

"No one cares about me, you and Max don't care about me, my own parents don't even care about me. And Gordon. Anyone who's ever been nice to me is not because I'm their friend, it's because they want something. You two wanted money to record your sketches, mum and dad wanted a nice well-educated daughter to marry off, Gordon wanted the script-"

"You wanted two actors for your movie you wanted to make, right? Listen, we all need each other. But that doesn't mean we're using each other."

"It's too late for the movie. What can we get done in a month?" asks Anisa.

"I have an idea," Chloe says.

Anisa and Max listen intently...

***

"So that's how the fake murder mystery begins. Chloe, Max and Anisa re-enact the Christmas do. We see some raw footage, courtesy of the mystery caller. I'll get back to him later," I say. "In the Christmas do re-enactment, when Anisa coughed up blood, she wasn't showing the tissue. Like the way Chloe showed hers when she was blowing her nose. And when it was in view, it was covered in blood."

"Ketchup, you mean," corrects Derek.

"Yeah, ketchup. It was all staged."

"Staged for revenge."

"Anisa faked her death, made it out as suspected murder. Chloe called the police station and reported. But it was a direct call to a particular person. Lyndsay. Chloe got Lyndsay on board with the plan and the fake murder mystery began."

"So if Anisa was recording our video calls as well, how come we didn't always see the red light flashing?" Derek asks me.

"Where did Anisa used to work? At an IT firm. She was able to record using the video call software and where necessary, she used other software to record our video calls without us even knowing," I reply.

"So she made her own film with this fake murder story. She was the director/actor, Max and Chloe were actors, and me and Gordon, without even knowing it, were also actors."

"Damn good ones, I tell you that," I can't help but say. "And the way the scenes were filmed and edited in the video footage we got. It switched between gallery and speaker views, that's something you won't normally do if you're in a meeting. It's something a director would do if they're filming a movie and want to capture their characters in particular shots. And Anisa did that for mine and Derek's video calls, whenever I accused Derek of messing around with the settings."

"And the filters, tell them about that filter Anisa put on you-"

"No I won't!"

Max joins in- "Hey Chloe, tell them about that filter Anisa put on you-"

"No I won't! Can we go now?!" asks Chloe.

"Be patient," I reply, "I'm sure Anisa wouldn't mind milking this final scene for a bit longer."

"I can't think of any gaps, you Max?" asks Chloe.

"No," Max replies. "Oh, uh, wait, I remember. The, uh, threats."

"As much as you wished they were staged, they weren't," Derek says.

"People send threats for anything," Chloe says.

"Just refund those people who paid for a gig that never happened."

"It did happen. For a few minutes. Anyway, I don't think we'll risk doing those gigs any time soon. Have to stick to virtual, for now."

"Appreciate it."

"Can we go now?" Chloe asks once again.

"Wait, wait," Derek says. "Gordon, why don't you finish off the scene by telling us who the mystery caller was."

"No problem," I say. "So, during this investigation, I had random calls from someone. They distorted their voice, and apparently they were able to spy through my camera. We referred to him as the mystery caller. I couldn't get an audio recording of his voice but when I played around with all your voices, there was only one that could match."

I play an audio file of the distorted voice.

"With distortion," I tell them.

I then play the file without the distortion. "Without distortion."

It was Anisa's voice all along.

"Okay, it was Anisa, what a surprise," Chloe says. Not really in a surprised way though. "So we now know everything was fake, I'm doing over-time already without getting paid, so me and Max will just leave-"

"The gig wasn't fake," says Derek. "And what was fake wasted my time and Gordon's time. So you, Max, Anisa. You all need to pay up."

"Pay up?" Anisa asks.

"Yeah, unpaid community service is an option, but let's face it, me and Derek acted our butts off in this film, we deserve something in return," I say.

"It wasn't acting because you believed it was all real," Anisa argues. "So it's more, reality TV."

"Still, reality TV stars get paid, don't they?"

"We can't pay you."

"Oh, so that part of the story about you being broke was real? And how about you leaving?"

"Can we just stop now?" Chloe asks, frustrated. "Anisa, come on."

Anisa leans forward, her finger about to land on the keys. "Alright, I'll stop recording."

There's one last thing I just have to say...

"Well that's an abrupt ending."

19

— • —

THE EXTRA BIT

Anisa's editing some scenes for the film while sharing her screen with Chloe.

"No, don't put that scene there," Chloe says.

"Why not?" asks Anisa.

"That's not the best take, play the other ones for that scene."

"We already looked through them, this is the best one."

"No it's not. I don't like the lighting."

"The lighting's the same in each one."

"No it's not. It took hours to film all these takes and towards the end, there was less natural light coming from the window."

"It's fine."

"Just play the other ones again."

Anisa sighs.

"I'm helping you out here, Anisa."

"Being bossy more like."

"You said something?"

"No."

Anisa finds the folder which has other takes of that scene.

"Play them all," says Chloe.

"No, I'm ignoring the first couple."

"But I do better in the first couple of takes-"

Anisa kicks Chloe out of the meeting.

Chloe's confused, thinking it's a mistake. "Anisa? Hello?"

***

"Angela says I can reduce the dose now," I tell Anisa on video call. "Hopefully in a few months, down to zero."

"Then forever at zero," reassures Anisa.

"You never know."

"Don't say that. If there's ever a dip again, we can always join that club."

"No, thanks. I learned a lot the last time."

"It won't happen again. Sorry."

"I just wanted to help you out."

"I know, I just didn't see that. When you're low, you see everything negatively. It's like wearing glasses that only let you see the blacks, the greys, all the dull things, you know?"

"Yeah I know."

I go to Derek's favourite window on the computer- the one with the filters.

I select his favourite sunglasses filter, with the black lens. "You're talking about these glasses, right?"

Anisa laughs.

***

My doorbell rings. Actual doorbell, by the way.

I answer.

It's Lyndsay. Wait, it's Lyndsay? Are my eyes deceiving me?

"Can I come in?" she asks.

"Uh, yeah."

I let Lyndsay into my, I mean our, lounge.

"It's tidy," Lyndsay says.

"Yeah, I hoover every couple of days now. Before it used to be, uh, never."

Lyndsay giggles, and sits down. I follow suit.

"How's things?" she asks me.

"Things are, actually good. Cases are coming in. Which is good, but also, you know, bad. Cos it means, there's crime. Basically, I'm busy again. But, good busy. Not bad, no work/life balance type busy."

"What about the film?"

"I agreed to let Anisa submit the film to that Virtual Filmfest, whatever it's called. Didn't win, but it got to the top three. Derek was praised for his comedy."

"Oh really?"

"Yeah, the guy loves his filters. Too bad filters don't work in the real world. It's December but he comes into the office sometimes with a pair of sunglasses on, you know, to cheer himself up."

"That's good."

"Chloe's getting some non-virtual acting jobs now. Some rap artist is collaborating with Max and using his stutter for one of his tracks. I heard it, it's actually quite good. Anisa got some funding to make another film. So, yeah. Everything is going great for everyone."

"And you?"

"Yeah, great for me too. Work's good. House is, tidy. Just feel a bit lonely sometimes."

"Me too."

"You have your sister and that little brat with you, how can you feel lonely?"

"Because I'm not with you, silly."

I smile.

"I figured I've tortured you enough. And to top things off, I was in cahoots with Chloe and Anisa on this fake murder mystery."

"Yeah, that was, um."

"I'm sorry. And I'm sure they apologised to you. It went too far."

"No, it's what I needed. I feel good now."

"And I got what I deserved, I guess. With the suspension. But you know what, I'm gonna quit. I want a change. Not that I want to get away from you in the office."

"I don't mind. Just don't get away from me 24/7. Please. I'm dying here."

Lyndsay smiles. And, as it would usually say at the end of a screen-play...

FADE TO BLACK.

Printed in Great Britain
by Amazon

45434210R00051